All-of-a-Kind Family
HANUKKAH

Based on the classic books
by Sydney Taylor

WRITTEN BY

EMILY JENKINS

ILLUSTRATED BY

PAUL O. ZELINSKY

schwartz & wade books · new york

When darkness comes, it will be the first night of Hanukkah, 1912.

Here on Henry Street, neighbors on New York's Lower East Side have set menorahs in the windows of the tenement buildings—but the candles are not yet lit.

"We'll have latkes tonight," says Gertie's sister Sarah. "With applesauce."

Gertie knows about latkes, but she can't remember how they taste. Mama makes the potato pancakes only on Hanukkah. The snow flies up when Gertie kicks it. Her boots make a rhythm on the sidewalk. She sticks out her tongue and eats a snowflake.

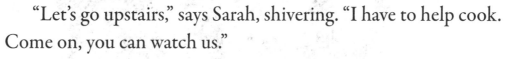

"Let's go upstairs," says Sarah, shivering. "I have to help cook. Come on, you can watch us."

"I don't want to watch," says Gertie. "I want to help, too. Please?"

"When Papa comes home," says Sarah, "we'll light the shamash and then the first candle on the menorah. Just that one candle, for the first night of Hanukkah."

"I know," says Gertie.

"Then we'll say the blessings in Hebrew."

"I know that, too!" says Gertie.

"We'll fry the latkes in schmaltz. Should I tell you why?
To remember the oil that burned for eight days and eight
nights in Jerusalem," says Sarah.

Gertie wants to say *I know* again, but she doesn't.

Her boots make a rhythm on the stairs.

Inside, a chicken roasts in the heavy iron oven. Carrots stand ready to be put in boiling water. Warm applesauce cools in a bowl.

By the time Gertie hangs up her coat, her four sisters are already at work.

Ella is twelve.   Henny is ten.

Sarah is eight.

Charlotte is six.

Gertie, who is four, thinks it is nice being all girls—"all of a kind," Papa and Mama like to say.

Charlotte is using a potato peeler. Long strips of potato skin drift onto a plate.

"Please can I help peel potatoes?" asks Gertie.

Charlotte hands over the peeler. "You have to press hard to get all the brown off."

"No, Mäusele," says Mama.
She gives the peeler back to Charlotte.
"It's too sharp."

Sarah has a bowl of peeled potatoes in cold water. She grates them into an even bigger bowl. The shreds have a sharp smell.

"Please can I have a turn?" Gertie asks.

"The grater is sharper than the peeler," says Mama. "Why don't you go look at the library book you brought home?"

No; it is special to make latkes.

Potatoes peeled, now potatoes grated. What's next? Henny is chopping onions with a heavy knife. Gertie knows Mama won't let her help with this one. "I wish I could chop," she says.

"No, you don't," says Henny, wiping her eyes. "Chopping onions is the worst of all the jobs. You're lucky. You don't have to do anything. You can just play all the time."

Potatoes peeled, then potatoes grated. Now onions chopped.

Gertie doesn't want to play.

Mama has cracked eggs
into a big china bowl,
without Gertie's help.
She sprinkles salt on top.
She shakes in matzo meal.
Potatoes peeled, then potatoes
grated and onions chopped. Now eggs,
salt, and matzo meal.
Mama stirs it all together.
"I wanted to help with the eggs." Gertie
goes over to big sister Ella at the stove. "Why
does Mama do everything without me?"

"You can help me," says Ella. "I'll pick you up."

Two big pans hiss with schmaltz. It smokes, and there are bubbles along the edges.

Mama comes over with the latke mixture. "Put her down now, Ella. When we fry, the grease could spit and burn her."

"I don't want to go down!"
shouts Gertie. "I want to help!"
Gertie's boots make a racket
on the kitchen floor.

Mama takes Gertie firmly by the hand. They
march to the bedroom.

"I will call you when it is time to say the blessings,"
Mama says quietly. "Until then, I don't want to hear
anything more."

The door closes behind Mama.
Gertie crawls under the bed she shares
with Charlotte and lies on her tummy.
   It is cold on the floor.
   They will miss her when they can't
find her.
   Mama will be sorry she didn't let
Gertie help. She will wish she'd been
nicer to her Mäusele.

But oh! The smells from the kitchen are good. Potatoes and onions fried in schmaltz. Latkes, rich and crispy.

Gertie can hear her sisters laughing as they set the table.
Now Ella is singing "Rock of Ages." Charlotte's voice joins in.
Will Mama ever call for Gertie?

Finally, the door creaks open.
Papa's feet appear by the bed.

"Pillow, where
is Gertie?" he asks.

Pillow says nothing.

"Library book, where is Gertie?" he asks.

Library book says nothing.

"Oh, handkerchief hidden under
the pillow and full of . . . gingersnaps.
Gingersnaps, you are not supposed
to be here. But do you know
where Gertie is?" asks Papa.
"Because I need her,
I must tell you."

Gertie can't help laughing. Papa is so funny.

"Wait. Is that Gertie I hear?" asks Papa. "Gingersnaps, why didn't you tell me?"

Papa reaches his hand under the bed. A gingersnap sits in his palm. Gertie takes it and pops it in her mouth.

"Come out, little one," says Papa. "It's Hanukkah."

All right. Gertie clambers out and puts her arms around Papa's neck, which is still cold from the out-of-doors.

"Am I glad to see you," says Papa. "I brought Uncle Hyman home with me. Do you want to come say hello?"

Gertie shakes her head.

"Mama said you had a hard day. Did you have a hard day?"

Gertie nods.

Papa thinks.

Then he says, "Tell me. Are you old enough to light the menorah this year?"

"Oh yes, Papa! I'm old enough," she says.

"Good. Because I need some help to kindle the lights of Hanukkah."

Darkness has come.
Mama smiles at Gertie when she
joins the family in the front room.
They set the menorah in the
window so the neighbors can see.
Everyone gathers round.

Papa strikes a match. He and Gertie
light the shamash, the helper candle.
    They say the blessings in Hebrew.
    And Gertie, together with Papa, takes
the shamash and lights the first candle,
just one candle, for the first night of
Hanukkah, for the first time.

The latkes have been kept hot in the oven. Mama gives the first one to Gertie.

Gertie gives a kiss to Mama.

The chicken is salty and the applesauce sweet.

The latkes taste of history and freedom, of love and crispy potato.

GLOSSARY

Please note that Yiddish is spoken in many dialects; the pronunciations given here are not the only correct ones.

latke (LAHT-kuh): A Yiddish word for a small potato pancake. Latkes are traditionally eaten during Hanukkah.

Mäusele (MOYZ-uh-luh): An old-fashioned, Yiddish-influenced German pet name meaning "little mouse."

menorah (men-AW-ra): A Hebrew word used in English for a nine-branched candleholder. It has one branch for each of the eight nights of Hanukkah, plus one for the shamash.

schmaltz (SHMOLTS): A Yiddish word for clarified poultry fat. Before the mid-twentieth century, schmaltz was used to fry latkes. Goose fat was best!

shamash (shah-MASH): A Hebrew word meaning "servant." The shamash is the helper candle on the menorah. It is lit first and used to light the others.

A NOTE FROM THE AUTHOR

Sydney Taylor (1904–1978) was born four years after her traditionally religious Jewish family arrived in America to settle on New York City's Lower East Side. Her parents, Morris and Cecilia, came from Germany, though Morris was originally from Poland. There were five girls, as in the All-of-a-Kind Family stories. Later, three boys were born, though only two survived.

As a young adult, the author changed her name from Sarah to Sydney. She grew up to be an actor and a modern dancer with the Martha Graham Dance Company. Later, she worked as a drama and dance counselor at a Jewish summer camp. As an adult, she was progressive and no longer observant, but she kept a strong Jewish identity.

In 1925, Sydney married Ralph Taylor. They had a daughter, Jo. "When Jo was little," Taylor said in *More Books by More People,* "I would sit beside her bed at night and try to make up for the lack of a big family by telling her about my own." Jo loved the stories, so Taylor wrote them down. One day, her husband secretly sent her manuscript to a contest sponsored by the Follett Publishing Company. She won.

All-of-a-Kind Family was published in 1951. Taylor became the first writer to publish books about Jewish children that reached readers from other religions. The books also gave Jewish children a mirror of their own traditions on the page.

The first book was so successful that Taylor wrote four sequels and a number of other books. The Sydney Taylor Book Award is now given every year by the Association of Jewish Libraries.

The **Lower East Side** of New York City was at one time the largest Jewish neighborhood in the world. Most of the immigrants there came from Germany, Russia, Poland, Romania, and Hungary. They spoke Yiddish. Others came from Greece, Turkey, and other parts of the Ottoman Empire. All of them had fled poverty and oppression to start new lives.

In 1912, housing in that area was mainly tenements: five- and six-story buildings, many of which had no running water. The all-of-a-kind family lives in an unusual two-story building.

The Lower East Side was a lively and culturally rich neighborhood, but overcrowding led to crime and disease. In *More Books by More People,* Taylor explained how it felt growing up there: "There was poverty, sickness, and unsanitary conditions, with the breadwinners working ten, twelve and fourteen hours a day for meager wages. But over and above all was the intoxicating joy in the freedom long denied the immigrants in their 'old countries.' . . . Here in this new land schools were free and libraries open to all."

Hanukkah, or the Festival of Lights, is one of many Jewish holidays in Taylor's books. It celebrates two miracles and happens over eight nights each year. Here is the story:

Long ago in Jerusalem, the Jewish people were ruled by Antiochus, a wicked king. He ordered the Jews to stop worshipping as they believed. A group led by Judah Maccabee fought back. Antiochus took over the Jewish temple. It looked as if there was no way Judah and his brothers could ever beat the king's huge army, but a miracle occurred: victory.

The Jews returned to their temple. They had to cleanse it in an eight-day ceremony, but oh no! There was only enough pure lamp oil to light the temple for one night. That's when a second miracle happened: that oil burned for all eight nights.

On Hanukkah, we put menorahs in windows to publicize these miracles. Money or *gelt* is a traditional Hanukkah gift for children. Kids also play dreidel, a spinning-top game. We eat fried foods like latkes and doughnuts because of the oil in the second miracle.

I grew up with Taylor's books and read them over and over. Now my children love them as much as I do.

My father is Jewish. His grandparents came to New York from Poland and Russia around the time Sydney Taylor was born. I was raised to remember this part of my family history. Now I share these books with my children as one of the ways we connect with our heritage. I am honored to have written a small chapter in the lives of Taylor's characters.

A Note from the Illustrator

The pictures I *intended* to draw for Emily's charming manuscript would reflect the popular esthetic of the 1910s: all lace and frills, meticulously detailed and decorated. But instead, my drawings came out quite loose and rough, as you can see. What happened?

It was largely about getting the feeling right. I quickly saw that delicate lines were wrong for Gertie's passionate nature; realistic space didn't reflect her sense of place in the world. Bolder outlines and simpler shapes, with almost no lighting or atmospherics, made the pictures ring truer—more like children's art, where the laws of perspective don't apply.

It was also about art. Though American illustration and popular art of the 1910s remained traditional, an art movement that would become known as Expressionism was growing in Europe and elsewhere, in which artists tried rough brushwork, wild perspective, and other strategies to heighten emotions in a way classical representation could not. I liked the idea of linking Gertie and her family to this budding world of creativity. Sydney Taylor's real family was deeply connected to art throughout their lives.

Now that I'm done, when I consider how I worked on these pictures, trying to rough them up when they got too smooth, to flatten them out when they got too round, to maintain a sense of texture throughout, I think that perhaps what I was really trying do was represent the qualities of a good potato latke! Take a look at one, very close up, and see if you agree.

Sydney Taylor's All-of-a-Kind Family Books

All-of-a-Kind Family (1951)
More All-of-a-Kind Family (1954)
All-of-a-Kind Family Uptown (1958)
All-of-a-Kind Family Downtown (1972)
Ella of All-of-a-Kind Family (1978)

For a link to additional back matter, including a latke recipe, visit AllofaKindFamilyHanukkahExtras.com.

For Ivy, who loved Taylor's stories even
more than I did, if that's possible —E.J.

For my own Löwinl, Deborah —P.O.Z.

ACKNOWLEDGMENTS

Many thanks to the Sydney Taylor Foundation and to Susan Cohen for enabling me to write this story. For help connecting me to resources, appreciation to Eva Kandel-Zasloff and Beth Zasloff of the Workmen's Circle, Catherine Lambrecht of the Culinary Historians of Chicago, author Deborah Heiligman, Elinor Grumet of the Hedi Steinberg Library, and my friend Laura Edidin. Thanks for historical expertise to anthropologist Ellen Steinberg, author of *Learning to Cook in 1898* and *From the Jewish Heartland*, among other books; Annie Polland, PhD, vice president of programs and education at the Lower East Side Tenement Museum; Laurie Tobias Cohen, director of the Lower East Side Jewish Conservancy; Professor June Cummins of San Diego State University, author of many articles on the All-of-a-Kind Family books; Marjorie Ingall, columnist for *Tablet* magazine; Serge Lippe, Senior Rabbi of the Brooklyn Heights Synagogue; and Tamar Rydzinski. Thanks to Colleen Fellingham for taking great care with the copyedit, and to my editor, Anne Schwartz, for the idea and for her guidance. All the gratitude in the world to Sydney Taylor for her wonderful stories.

SOURCES

Berenbaum, Michael, and Fred Skolnik, eds. *Encyclopedia Judaica,* 2nd ed. Vol. 19. Detroit: Macmillan Reference USA, 2007.

Bloom, Susan. "Sydney Taylor." In *The Jewish Women's Archive Encyclopedia.* Accessed February 16, 2016. http://jwa.org/people/taylor-sydney.

Cummins, June. "Becoming an 'All-of-a-Kind' American: Sydney Taylor and Strategies of Assimilation." *The Lion and the Unicorn* 27, no. 3 (September 2003): 324–43.

Cummins, June. "Leaning Left: Progressive Politics in Sydney Taylor's All-of-a-Kind Family Series." *Children's Literature Association Quarterly* 30, no. 4 (Winter 2005): 386–408.

Cummins, June. "Sydney Taylor: A Centenary Celebration." *The Horn Book,* March 30, 2005. Accessed February 16, 2016. hbook.com/2005/03/authors-illustrators/sydney-taylor-centenary-celebration.

Estrin, Heidi R., ed. *The All-of-a-Kind Family Companion.* The Association of Jewish Libraries, 2004. Accessed February 16, 2016. http://jewishlibraries.org/images/downloads/Sydney_Taylor_Book_Award/companion.pdf.

Heiligman, Deborah. *Celebrate Hanukkah with Lights, Latkes, and Dreidels.* Washington, DC: National Geographic, 2006.

Hopkins, Lee Bennett. *More Books by More People.* New York: Citation Press, 1974.

Lehman-Wilzig, Tami. *Hanukkah Around the World.* Illustrated by Vicki Wehrman. Minneapolis: Kar-Ben Publishing, 2009.

Lippe, Serge. "Conversation about Hanukkah and Jewish Traditions." Personal interview by the author, Brooklyn Heights Synagogue, February 24, 2016.

Lower East Side Tenement Museum. "All of a Kind Family—Tenement Talk from 2014" [sic]. Accessed February 16, 2016. https://www.youtube.com/watch?v=yzN4CfbTQXg.

Polland, Annie. "Conversation about the History of the Lower East Side." Email discussion with the author, February 27, 2016.

Steinberg, Ellen. "Conversation about Food Preparation and Jewish Practices in 1912." Email discussion with the author, February 12, 2016.

"Sydney Taylor," Jewish Virtual Library. The American-Israeli Cooperative Enterprise, 2012. Accessed February 16, 2016. jewishvirtuallibrary.org/jsource/judaica/ejud_0002_0019_0_19654.html.

Tobias Cohen, Laurie. "Conversation about the History of Jewish People on the Lower East Side." Telephone conversation with the author, February 21, 2016.